Emmett

Dear Emmett,

You *are everything* to me! From your smile to your laugh to your giggles and toes, I simply can't imagine life without you. Here's a story to help you understand just how precious you *are*—and what Everything really means.

Love,

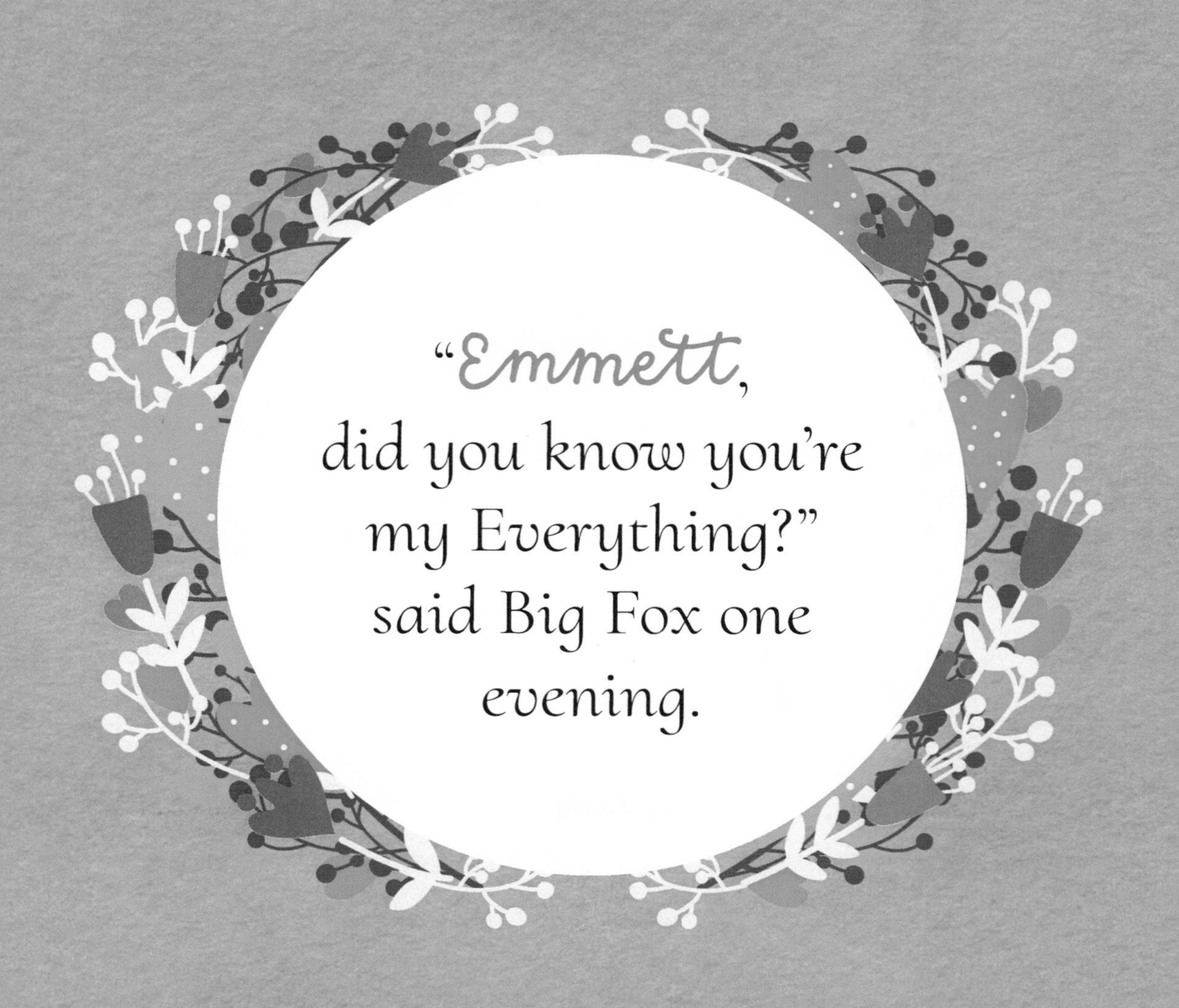
"Emmett,
did you know you're
my Everything?"
said Big Fox one
evening.

"You tell me all the time!" said Emmett.
"But what *is* Everything?"

"Oh, Everything is
the best thing you
could be. It's every
new flower that
blooms in spring."

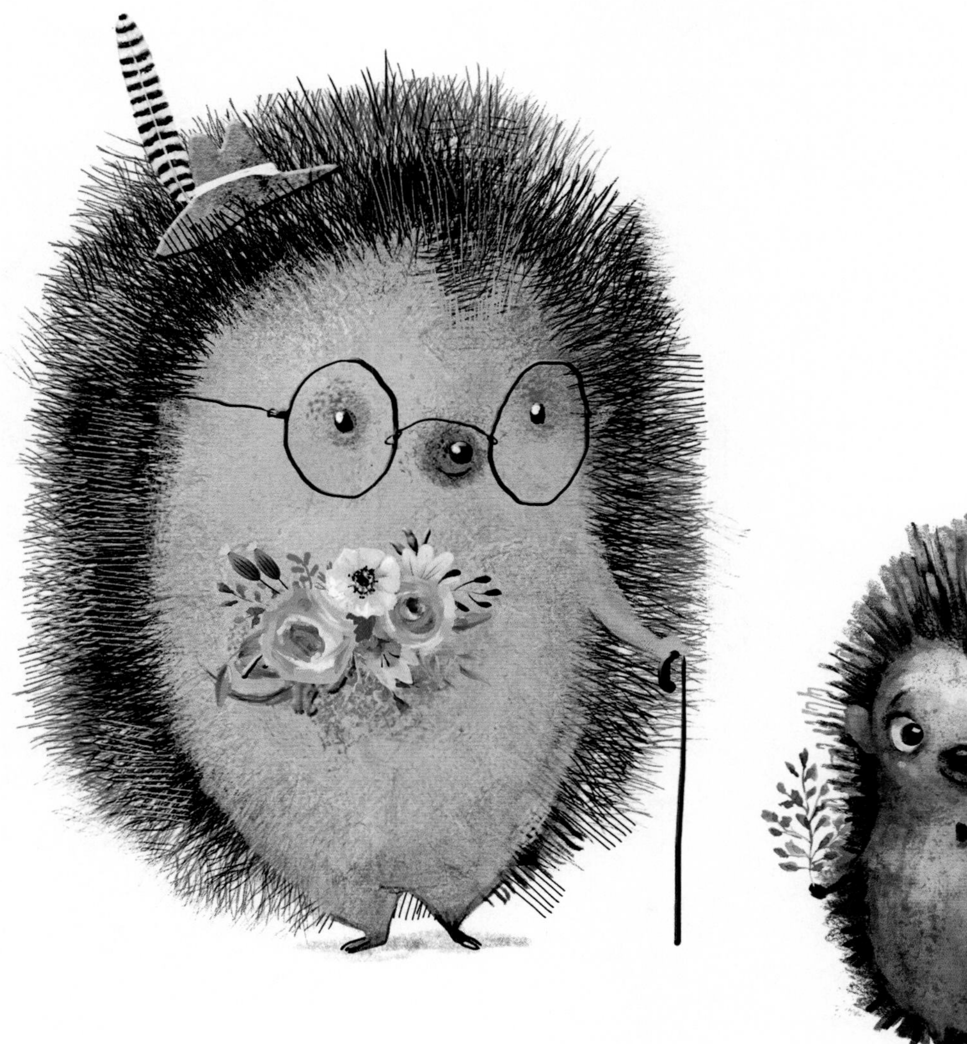

"And every drop of rain that cools the summer."

"It's what it feels
like to ride down
the longest hill
in the world. "

"Or to float up to
the highest clouds
in the sky."

"Everything is *warmer* than the softest penguin in the snow."

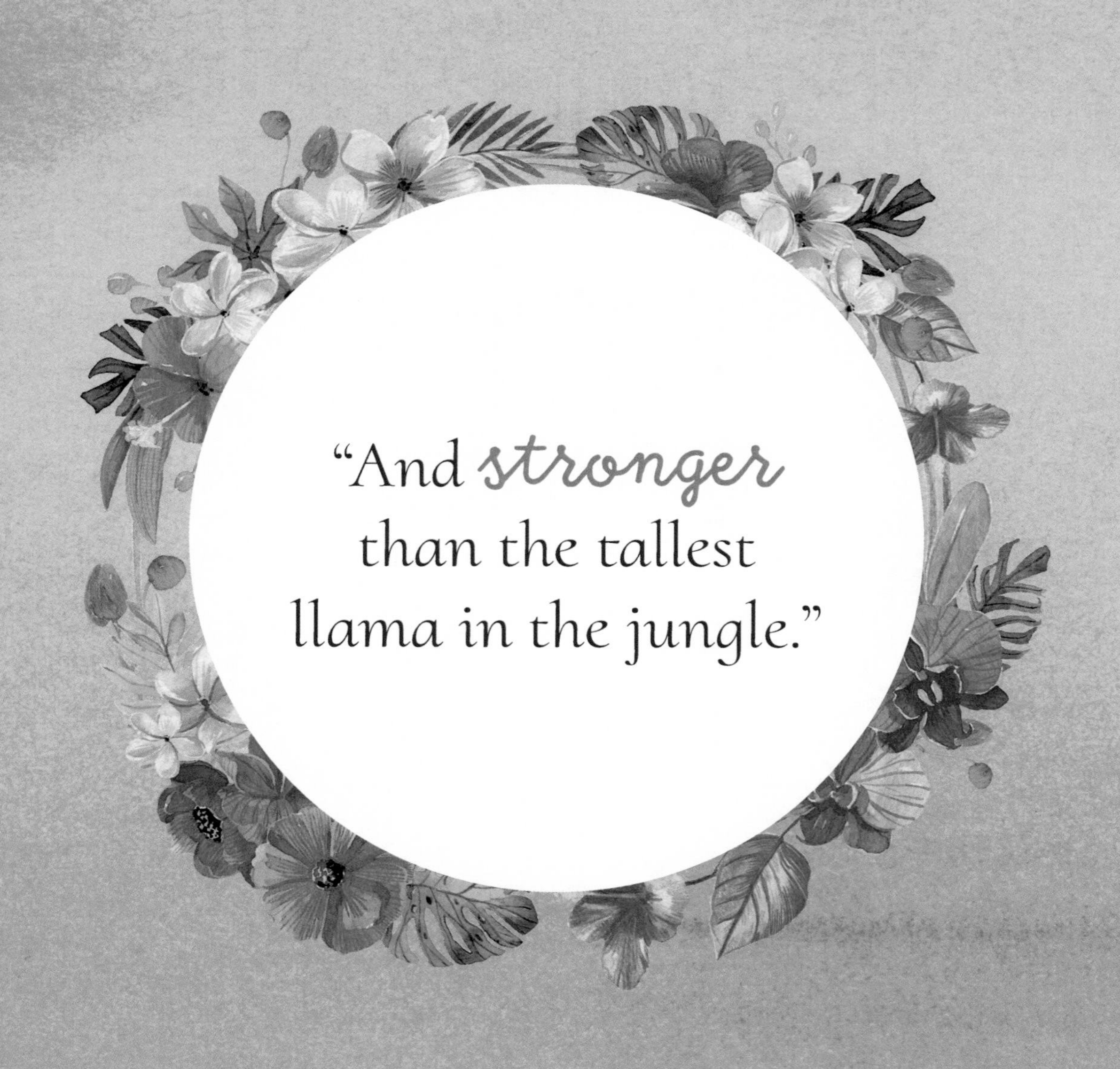

"And *stronger*
than the tallest
llama in the jungle."

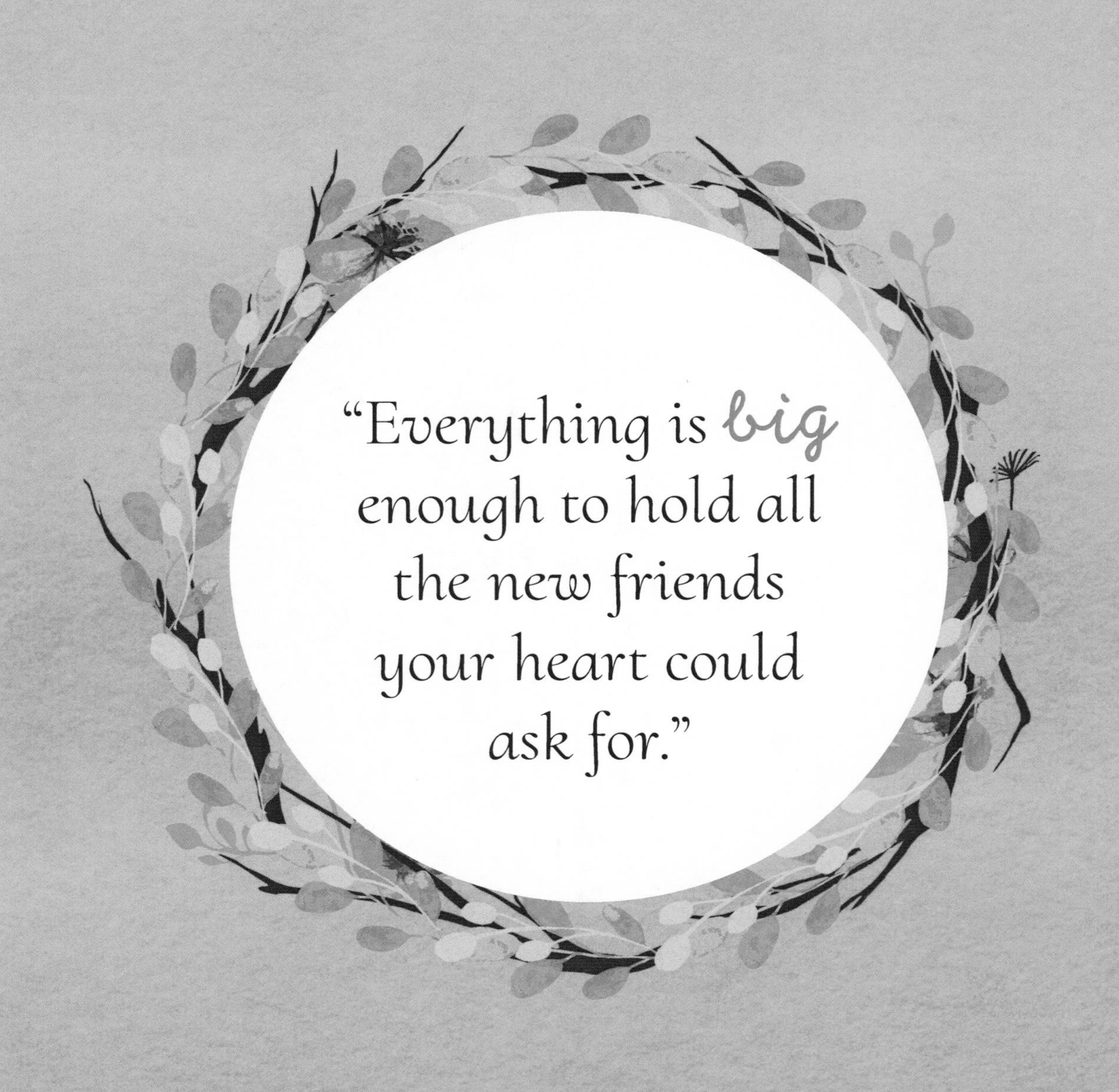
"Everything is big
enough to hold all
the new friends
your heart could
ask for."

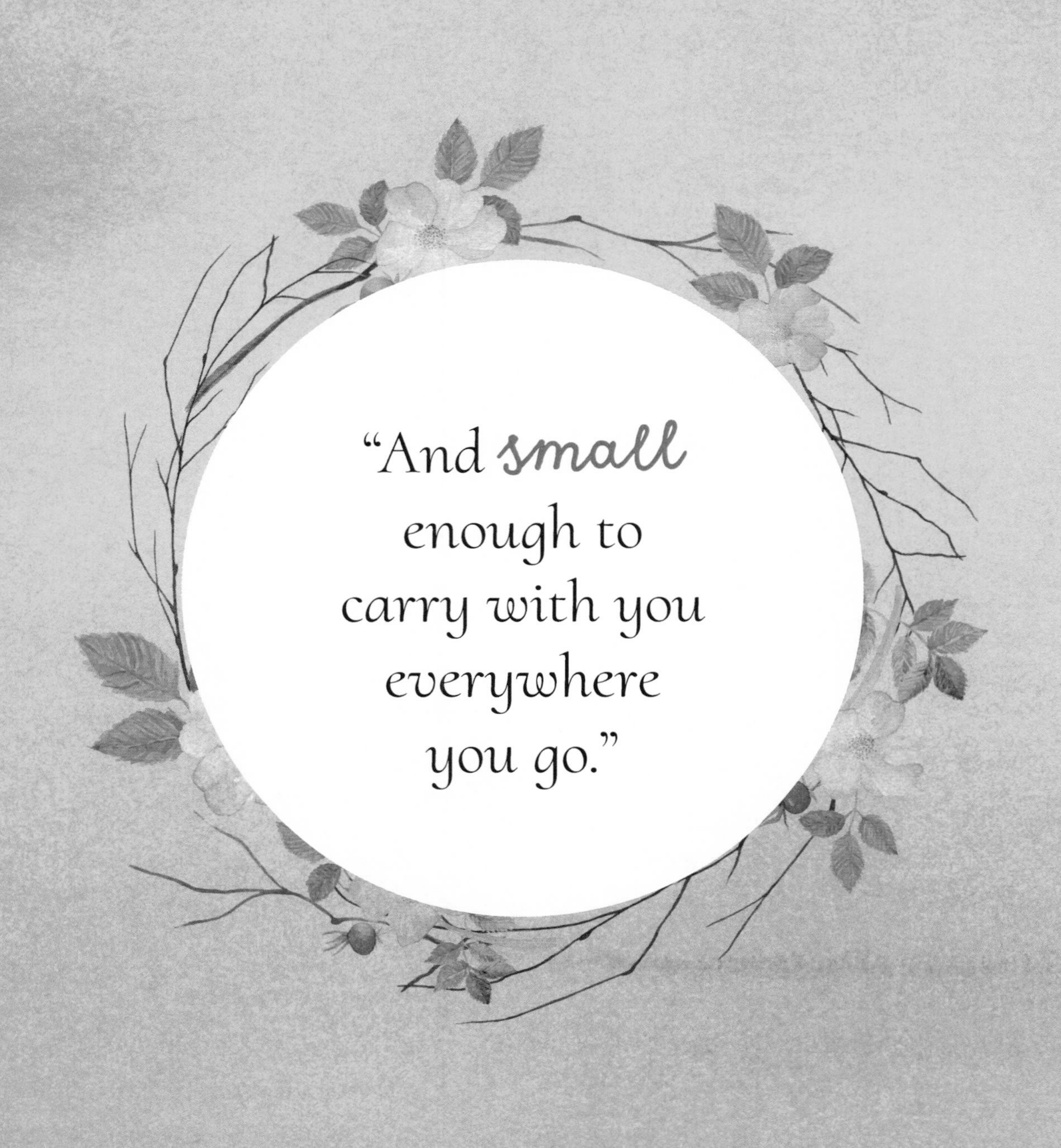
"And small
enough to
carry with you
everywhere
you go."

"Everything means,
'I love you with all
my heart.' On your
happy days . . ."

". . . and on your
hard days."

"And it means I
will always be
there during the
long, long nights."

"Best of all,
Everything lasts
forever—longer,
even, than the longest
story that was ever
written."

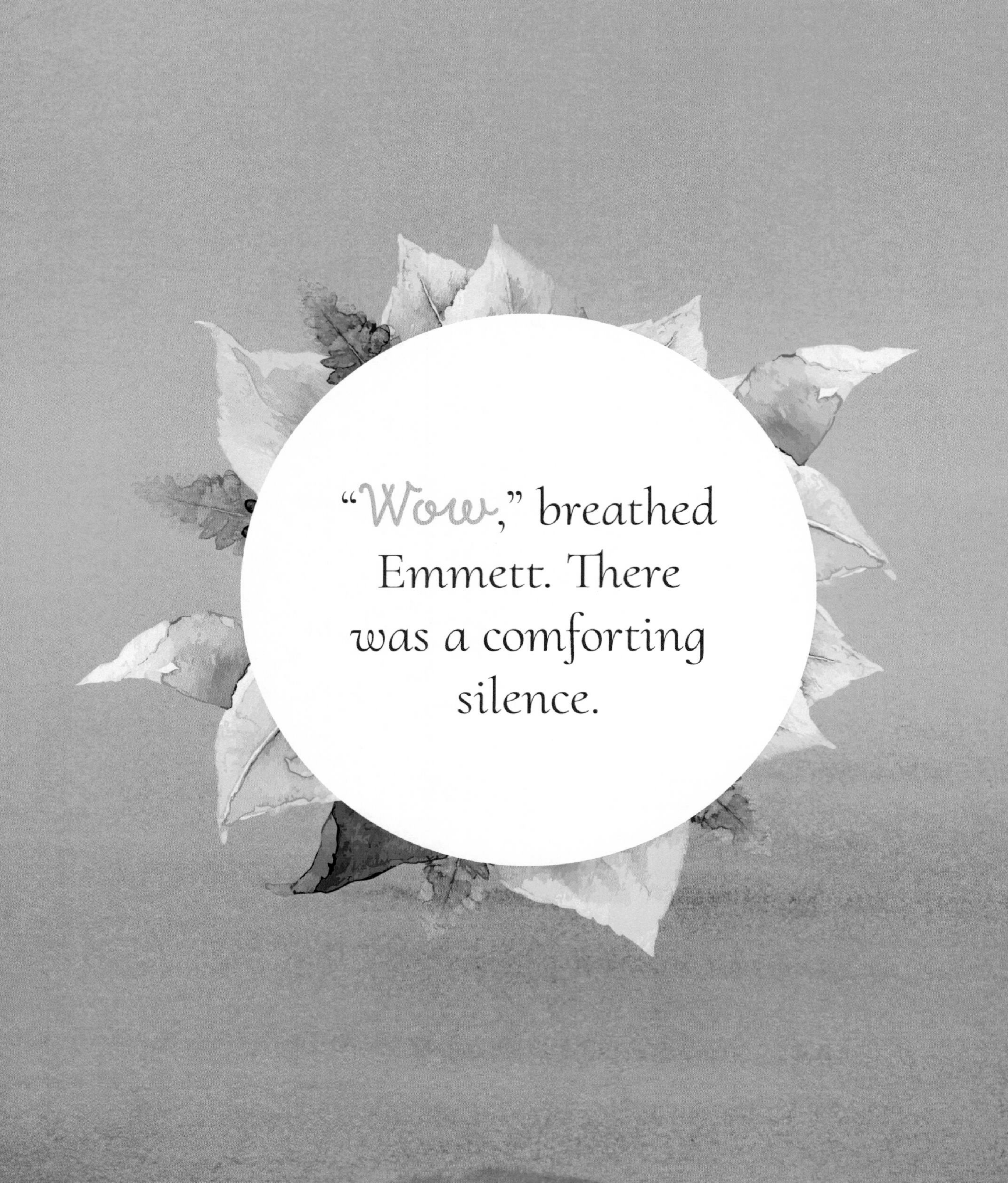

"*Wow*," breathed Emmett. There was a comforting silence.

Then Emmett whispered, "If Everything means all that, then *you're* my Everything, too."

Dearest Emmett, you are my Everything in so many ways! Here are just a few:

Cover and book design by David Miles

Visual credits: animal illustrations (Elena Barenbaum/Shutterstock.com); pink and green flower border (Karma3/Shutterstock.com); green leaves border (mika48/Shutterstock.com); colorful flower border (oksanka007/Shutterstock.com); yellow daisy flower border (TonTonic/Shutterstock.com); blue flower border (elsabenaa/Shutterstock.com); poppy flower border (OlgaVinokurova_art/Shutterstock.com); rose hip and twig flower border (Eisfrei/Shutterstock.com); fall flower border (Gluiki/Shutterstock.com); tropical flower border (Yana Fefelova/Shutterstock.com); snowflake border (Tokarchuk Andrii/Shutterstock.com); balloon border (Anastasia Lembrik/Shutterstock.com); apple flower border (julagaladriel/Shutterstock.com); raindrop border (Xansa/Shutterstock.com); red and blue flower border (Qvasimodo art/Shutterstock.com); clouds (Anna Konchits/Shutterstock.com); water puddle (Cute art/Shutterstock.com); cover stars (Margarita Manish/Shutterstock.com); cover star background (Anna Kutukova/Shutterstock.com); purple, red, and orange watercolor background (Jolliolly/Shutterstock.com); green and blue streaked watercolor background (Jolliolly/Shutterstock.com); green and blue watercolor background (Rennes/Shutterstock.com); cloud watercolor background (Magenta10/Shutterstock.com); blue watercolor background (Alyushin/Shutterstock.com); yellow and orange watercolor background (foxie/Shutterstock.com).

Made in United States
North Haven, CT
28 September 2022